**The twin stars
of this book are:**

_____ and _____

who answered our wishes on:

_____

For Grace and Myla.
You sparkle in our hearts.

All rights reserved. Published in the United States by Doubleday, an imprint of
Random House Children's Books, a division of Penguin Random House LLC, New York.

Doubleday and the colophon are registered trademarks of Penguin Random House LLC.

Visit us on the Web! rhcbooks.com

Educators and librarians, for a variety of teaching tools, visit us at RHTeachersLibrarians.com

Library of Congress Cataloging-in-Publication Data
Name: Rohner, Dorothia, author.
Title: A wish for twins : the tale of our two miracles / by Dorothia Rohner.
Description: New York : Doubleday Books for Young Readers, [2022] | Audience: Ages 0-3 |
Summary: "This celebration of twins posits the magical idea that twins are made of stardust, floating sweetly
in the celestial heavens until they find each other and are called to Earth to meet their family." —Provided by publisher.
Identifiers: LCCN 2021021153 (print) | LCCN 2021021154 (ebook) |
ISBN 978-0-593-48197-4 (hardcover) | ISBN 978-0-593-48198-1 (library binding) | ISBN 978-0-593-48199-8 (ebook)
Subjects: CYAC: Twins—Fiction. | Fantasy.
Classification: LCC PZ7.1.R6645 Wi 2022 (print) | LCC PZ7.1.R6645 (ebook) | DDC [E]—dc23

MANUFACTURED IN CHINA
10 9 8 7 6 5 4 3 2 1
First Edition

A WISH FOR TWINS

The Tale of Our Two Miracles

By Dorothia Rohner

Doubleday Books for Young Readers

You once twinkled in the stars,

crisscrossed the cosmos, before and beyond.

You sailed through stardust,
twirled across time.

For light-years you traveled—

star-hopped alone.

Until . . .

. . . one magic moment

. . . destiny dawned.

You bonded in kinship, swung from the stars.

Forever together—
two kindred souls.

You skipped moonstones with Centaur

lingered with Lion,

caught the tail of a comet.
Through galaxies you glided.

You hopscotched the heavens,

reveled with Ram,

swam deep space with Fishes,

caught quasars with Crab.

You skated the rings that swirl around Saturn.

You dreamed of . . .

voices that hummed
as you drifted to sleep,

kisses and hugs
that filled you with peace,

story time cuddled up
close with a book,

wondrous discoveries beyond your belief.

You imagined a family, a place to call home.

You heard us wish
when we wished on a star

from the pale blue dot,
our home, planet Earth.

The planets aligned on the day you were born.

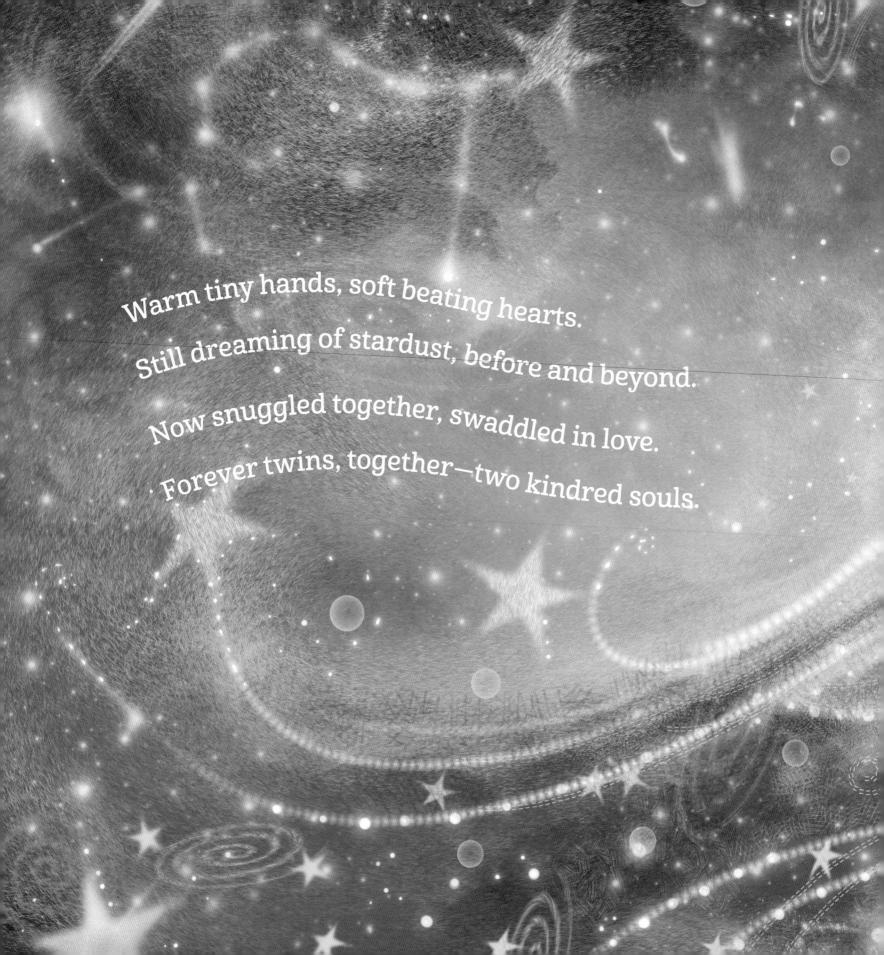

Warm tiny hands, soft beating hearts.
Still dreaming of stardust, before and beyond.

Now snuggled together, swaddled in love.
Forever twins, together—two kindred souls.

You once twinkled in the stars.

Now you sparkle in our hearts.

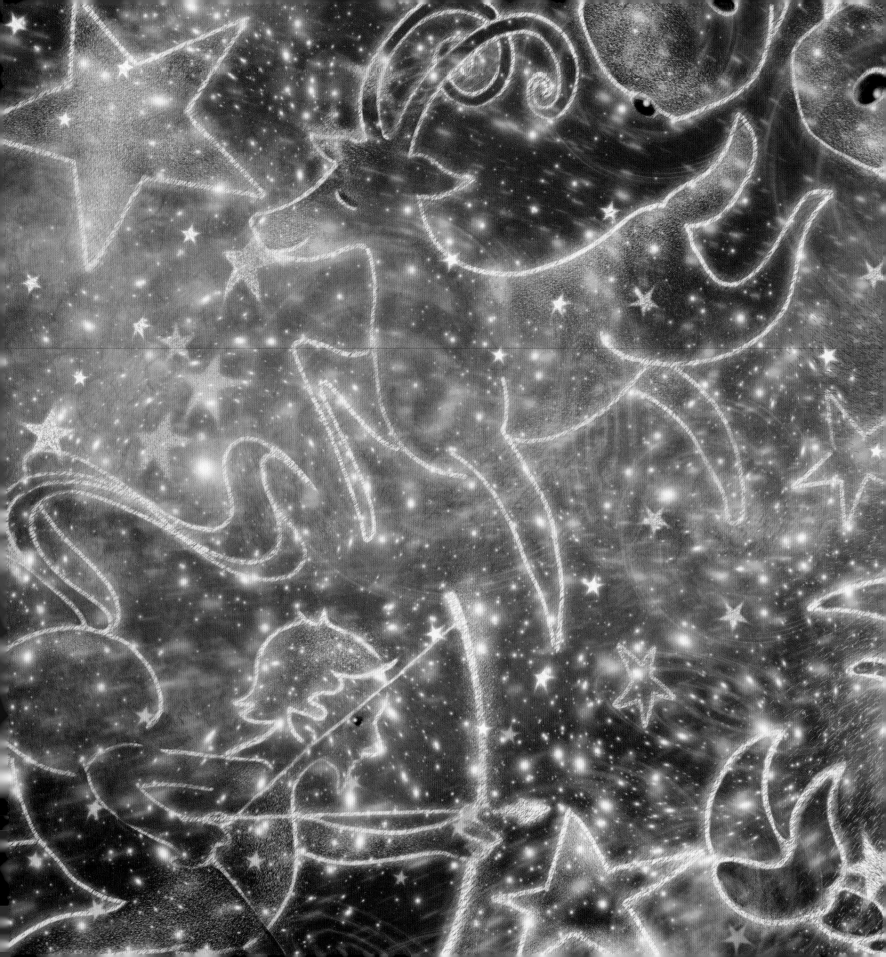